Spider

Written by Ratu Mataira

Look at this spider.

Where can this
spider live?

It can live
in the garden.

garden

3

Where can this
spider live?

It can live
in a hole.

4

Where can this
spider live?

This spider can live
in a hole, too.
It can go
in and out.

hole

Where can this
spider live?

It can live
in a web.
The babies are
in the web, too.

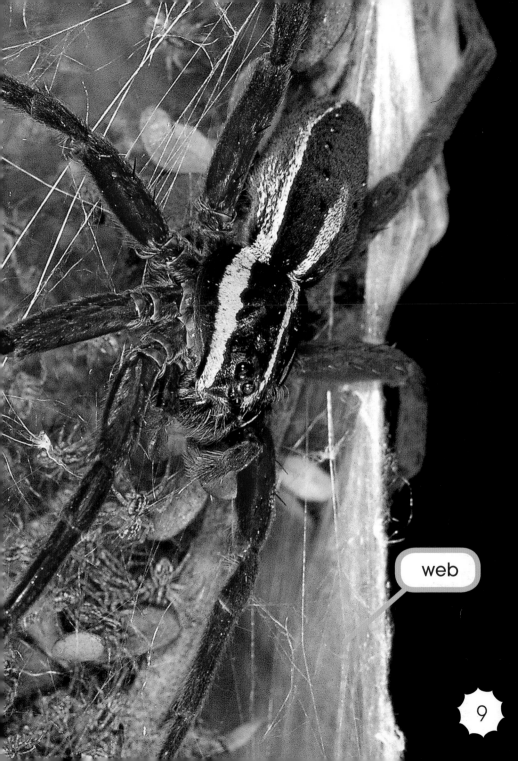

web

Where can this
spider live?

This spider can
live in the water.
It is in a bubble.

This spider can live **on** the water.

water

Where spiders live:

web

in water

on water

garden

Index

holes

15

Guide Notes

Title: Spider Homes
Stage: Early (1) – Red

Genre: Nonfiction
Approach: Guided Reading
Processes: Thinking Critically, Exploring Language, Processing Information
Written and Visual Focus: Photographs (static images), Index, Labels
Word Count: 90

THINKING CRITICALLY
(sample questions)
- Look at the title and read it to the children.
- Tell the children this book is about some places that spiders live.
- Ask them what they know about where spiders live.
- Focus the children's attention on the index. Ask: "What are you going to find out about in this book?"
- If you want to find out about spider homes in a garden, which page would you look on?
- If you want to find out about spider homes in a hole, which pages would you look on?
- Look at the spider on page 11. How do you think it can stay alive in the
- Where do you think might be the safest place for a spider to live?

EXPLORING LANGUAGE

Terminology
Title, cover, photographs, author, photographers

Vocabulary
Interest words: spider, hole, bubble, water, garden, web
High-frequency words: it, where
Positional words: in, on, out

Print Conventions
Capital letter for sentence beginnings, periods, comma, question marks